For Brian

Chapter One

I couldn't catch my breath. This was the scariest part yet! Mary had just opened the tapestry-covered door and discovered a little boy, crying in his bed.

"Who are you?" the boy asked Mary. "Are you a ghost?"

"No, I am . . . "

"Amy! Amy Fay Jones!"

"Wha-?" I practically jumped out of my seat. My library book went flying. It hit the top of the school bus with a *thump* and crashed back into my lap.

"Oh no!" I yelled. "I lost my place!"

Mary and the boy and everything else about my book, "The Secret Garden," poofed away in an instant.

Instead, I found myself staring into the grinning face of William Mott. He was hanging over the seat in front of me.

"You better get your nose out of that book, Amy," William teased. "We almost at your stop!" His blond crew cut stood up on his head like a thatch of corn stalks from my Daddy's fields.

"Don't know why you bother," he continued.

1

"Hit's not even on the sixth grade reading list. You sure are dumb to do work you don't have to!"

I rolled my eyes and tried to ignore him.

I hated William. He teased me every day. It was like riding the bus with your little brother!

He even *looked* like my kin. We both had the same straight blond hair. We each had light blue eyes. We were both real skinny. And we both had the kind of pale skin that got red and freckled after about five minutes in the sun.

It was a Monday afternoon and we were heading home to Bearhead Holler. The gravel road was rough with pits and potholes. But I was used to the bumpy ride. All my twelve-year-old life, that's how the roads have been in our neck of the Appalachian Mountains in eastern Kentucky. Poor.

In any case, dopey ol' William hadn't been teasing about one thing. My stop was right around the next curve.

The bus lurched to a halt and all us kids from Bearhead Holler headed up the aisle. I am happy to say we didn't include William, who lived one holler over from mine. I sneered at him as I passed.

"Smell ya later, William," I called. "And do I mean *smell*!" I pinched my nose, laughed loudly and jumped off the bus.

I landed hard. *Ow!* A sharp stone stabbed me in the big toe.

I looked down at my shoes — cheap ol' Wal-Mart sneakers that were falling apart. The duct tape I used to patch them hardly did any good.

A cold breeze was blowing, flapping my hand-me-down skirt and raggedy T-shirt. Underneath my T-shirt, my stomach was growling. All I'd had for lunch was a couple of biscuits and an apple. No ham. No cheese, even. Mama said we were having a tough month.

Again.

I sighed and began to walk up the dirt road that cut through the holler to my house. I lived at the far end of the holler, so I had a long haul home.

While I walked, I thought of Mary in "The Secret Garden." Even though she was an orphan, Mary was still rich. She had lots of beautiful clothes, and servants to dress her, even! A massive mansion. And a secret garden! A place all her own, overflowing with flowers and, I bet, sweet things to eat.

I sighed again and trudged along. I was tired. I was hungry. I wanted to cry out, "Why, oh why, am I so poor?"

Chapter Two

A holler is just what it sounds like — a hollow, bowl-shaped patch of land that rests in the middle of a bunch of mountains. Hidden among the hills in these parts are a whole lot of them — Camp Creek Holler, Lame Bird Holler, Huckleberry Holler, and others.

Hollers are where most mountain people live. Since the coal mines closed, a lot of folks try to scratch a living out of their tired soil, or they become lumber men, or they drive to Lexington to work in factories. Like my older brother Jud, who works the night shift at a textile mill.

'Course, a lot of my friends down the holler have only a welfare check to survive on. They live in rickety trailers planted among the trees. Or in shacks with tarpaper roofs.

My daddy farms. Or at least he tries to. He says pollution from the old coal mines and erosion from cutting down too many trees has made our soil as dusty as a desert.

Daddy's corn stalks are spindly. Half the potatoes, tomatoes and beans he plants turn sour. We only have enough grazing land to keep two cows.

Still, because he can't find any other work,

Daddy tries. That's just what he was doing when I finally caught sight of our house. He was crouched in the turnip field, picking rocks out of the soil furrows.

"Hey Daddy," I called out, waving.

He just grunted.

I trudged up the porch steps. Compared to some of my friends, I'm pretty lucky when it comes to my house. We live in a sturdy log cabin my great-granddaddy built around the turn of the century.

It's not fancy. We only have pump water, and a couple electrical outlets. But the house stays pretty warm, and the tin roof keeps the rain out.

My mamaw (that's what all Appalachian folks call their grandmothers) was born here. And she lives here still, with me, Mama, Daddy and Jud.

Right now, Mama and Mamaw were sitting on the porch. Mama was popping beans over a cracked bowl. She nodded at me and the cigarette dangling from her lips bobbled a little bit. But she didn't bother to say hello or offer me an after-school snack.

"How are ya, Mama?" I asked. "Jud at work already?"

She grunted a yes.

I kneeled next to my grandmother's rocker.

"Mamaw? Mamaw, I'm home from school," I said softly.

Mamaw barely turned her leathery ninety-year-old face towards me. Her blue eyes were cloudy.

But Mamaw wasn't blind. She was just, well, not quite there.

"Are you the preacher?" she quavered.

"No, Mamaw," I said sadly. "I'm Amy. I'm your granddaughter."

I went into the house. Clutching "The Secret Garden" under one arm, I crawled up the steps to the loft, which doubles as a bedroom for Mamaw and me.

I read by the fading light that came through the window until Mama called me for dinner.

Chapter Three

"Betty, you've got to get some food in you!" my mama said, shoving a spoonful of mashed potatoes at Mamaw's closed mouth.

"I only eat my daughter-in-law's cooking," Mamaw hissed through clenched lips.

"I *am* your daughter-in-law," Mama protested.

"No you ain't," Mamaw croaked.

She wouldn't take a bite. My grandma's delusions were growing as fast as her appetite was dwindling.

Daddy growled angrily and shoveled in his meager dinner.

A sullen silence hung over our table. The quiet felt heavier than the smells of Mama's fried pork chops and stewed tomatoes.

As I gnawed on my tough meat, my eyes wandered to the log wall. Stuck carelessly in a tin frame was a photo I'd almost forgotten.

It was Mamaw as a little girl.

She looked to be about my age. But she was plump and happy. Her hair hung in long, brown corkscrews. She sat grinning on the front steps of this very house. She was surrounded by her parents and a whole crew of rosy-cheeked uncles and aunts and cousins.

They sure look a sight happier than we are here today, I thought. Healthier, too.

Mamaw's dress was snowy white. Her mother didn't have gray circles under her eyes like mine did. She looked relaxed, fat and contented.

"Wow," I burst out. "From the looks of that picture, I'd say Mamaw was almost rich when she was little."

"Naw," Daddy scoffed.

But Mamaw seemed to sit up a little straighter. She looked at me! I could swear she was trying to say something. But no sound came out of her trembling lips.

Mamaw *used* to talk all the time. She would tell me about Papaw, her husband, who had died when I was just a baby. And about the way the hollers bustled with life when the mines were still open — back when coal was king.

When I was ten, Mamaw and I had made a crazy quilt together. While we sewed tiny stitches in the mismatched scraps of fabric, she'd weave fairy tales.

She told stories about a long-lost family fortune. She talked about a black treasure buried beneath the foundation of our house. And diamonds under our very own feet!

But nobody else in my family ever talked about the fortune.

Only Mamaw.

And she couldn't make sense anymore.

I *had* to know.

"What do you know about our fortune?" I blurted out. "Great-granddaddy's fortune. The treasure Mamaw used to talk about?"

Daddy scowled. Mama laid down her spoonful of potatoes, looking exhausted.

"There ain't no fortune; you know that Amy," Mama said. "That was just Mamaw's talk."

I pointed at the photo. "But she said . . . "

"Listen to your Mama," Daddy interrupted. His face went red, and he jumped to his feet and gripped the edge of the table.

"Daddy, I'm sorr- . . . " I started to say in a trembling voice.

He cut me off, roaring, "If there was some family fortune, we'd all be doing a sight better, wouldn't we? Now, if you want to babble any more of this nonsense, you can just get yourself up from this table and go to bed early!"

Chapter Four

It was almost midnight.

I had been in bed all evening, sulking and reading by the light of my kerosene lamp. I was just drifting off to sleep when Mamaw stirred in her bed on the other side of the loft.

"Mamaw?" I said, peering at my grandmother's tormented face.

"Water," she croaked.

I dashed downstairs and used the kitchen pump to draw Mamaw some cool water.

She drank the whole glass. It seemed to calm her. She even opened her mouth, as if to speak.

I dropped to my knees beside her bed and leaned forward. "What Mamaw?" I breathed. "What is it?"

But Mamaw turned her tired face to the wall.

"Mamaw, please," I said. "Please tell me your secret. What happened to our family? Our fortune? Why are we so miserable?"

Mamaw didn't — or *couldn't* — answer. I couldn't take it anymore. Sobs leapt from my throat. I hid my face in Mamaw's quilts.

I cried until I couldn't anymore. Then I slept, curled up on the rag rug next to my Mamaw's motionless form.

Chapter Five

Mamaw got worse.

On Tuesday, she stopped talking. By Thursday, she'd stopped eating. We couldn't even get her out of bed.

By Saturday morning, I was really scared. And frustrated.

I stomped onto the front porch. Daddy was whittling, dropping shavings in a pile on the floor.

When Daddy took to woodcarving, he went off in his own world. There was no talking to him.

I stomped back inside and turned on our black and white TV. Up here, we only got two stations. On the first station was football. Blech! I flipped the channel. The Frugal Gourmet? "Argh!"

"Amy!" Mama snapped, poking her head out of the loft.

"Whoops," I called. "I thought that 'argh' was just in my head."

"Young lady, you are het up!" Mama said sharply. "I know you're worried about Mamaw. But there's nothing you can do."

She stopped for a minute, then continued.

12

"Actually, there *is* something you can do," she said. "Why don't you go get some fresh air? We don't need you stomping around the house making everybody nervous."

I grabbed my library card and flounced out of the house. As I stalked down the dirt road towards the bottom of Bearhead Holler, I wiped away angry tears.

Mama was so mean!

But a few steps later, I realized she was right. There was nothing I *could* do to help my Mamaw. I was worthless!

I felt so bad, I didn't even want to go meet the bookmobile. And I *never* miss the bookmobile's Saturday visits to Bearhead Holler.

When I got to the bus stop, which is also the bookmobile stop, I kept going.

I was walking aimlessly up the main road when the bookmobile drove up.

"You're going the wrong way!" called the driver. It was Bo the Book Man. At least, that's what everyone called him.

Bo wore thick, black-rimmed glasses. He was about six and a half feet tall and all bones. He stooped because he was too big for the bookmobile. And he always seemed to be tittering through his long, pointy teeth.

Here's the thing about Bo the Book Man — he had a sixth sense about kids and books. He would look you up and down. He would peer into your eyes. Then he'd gently lead you to the perfect book, hidden somewhere on the dusty shelves.

But today, I just didn't have the heart to choose a new book. Or to chat with Bo.

"I'm not coming today," I said.

"What? And break a three-year streak?" Bo exclaimed. "I don't think I can allow that!"

"I'm just not in the mood," I insisted.

Bo looked me up and down. He peered into my eyes. Then he said seriously, "I think there may be something for you here today. Something you wouldn't want to miss. Why don't you hop in?"

Something in the way Bo *didn't* titter through his yellow teeth convinced me. I climbed into the bookmobile. Bo drove the short distance to our bus stop, where a small crowd of my Bearhead neighbors was waiting.

As they clambered on board, Bo winked at me. He pointed to the back of the bookmobile with a long, bony finger.

"At the *very* back?" I squeaked. "B-b-but, I never go back there. The light's been burnt out forever. And it's full of cobwebs!"

Bo just winked again. And pointed again.

"Go!" he hissed.

I went.

I crept past my usual hangout, the Young Adult section. I passed the newspaper and magazine rack where a bunch of grown-ups were gossiping. I slunk through History, Biography and War Studies.

I took a deep breath. Then I sidled into the last

14

nook. A dead light bulb swung from a cord over my head. The shelves were veiled in shadows. The section was labeled, "Travel/Vacation/Occult."

"What a weird combination," I whispered. I inched down the aisle.

A cobweb brushed across my face. I clapped my hands over my mouth to keep from shrieking.

But the books themselves? Well, they were far from spine-tingling. Or even interesting.

One was called, "See Rock City!" Another was "A Guide to Your Country's Rest Areas."

"Oh puh-leeze," I muttered. "This is no big deal after all."

I started flipping through the rest of the books. Most were thin paperbacks.

Then I stopped. A shiver skittered through me. I was staring at a massive leather book.

It was tall.

It was thick.

It was heavy.

Its spine was made of cracked, tea-colored leather. And it was so dusty that I couldn't read the title.

With a trembling finger, I reached down and swiped away a gob of grime. Underneath the dust were gold, gothic-style letters. But they didn't seem to spell out anything except gibberish.

At least at first!

Suddenly, before my very eyes, the letters began to arrange themselves into a different order.

I stared in awe. And when complete words finally formed, I gasped with surprise.

Chapter Six

"Hillbilly Witchery: Proceed At Your Own Risk," the gold letters read.

I gulped. I watched my hand shake as it reached for the book.

The chatter of the folks crowding the front of the bookmobile drifted away. It was as if I was in a cave, all alone, when I cracked opened the heavy, leather volume.

The book's grainy onionskin paper gave me the chills.

On the first page, I saw the book's subtitle: "Myths, Legends and Spells. Seek Power. See the World. *Be Who You Are Not!*"

Underneath that was a date: 1916.

"Wow, it's *ancient*," I whispered.

I shivered.

As I flipped through the pages, I noticed something funny. The letters seemed to squiggle into words only a split second before my eyes fell on them!

For some reason, I barely paused to study these strange pages. I flew past ancient stories about life in eastern Kentucky. I ignored tales of slave rebel-

17

lions and family feuds.

As if my hand were controlled by some invisible puppeteer, I kept skimming through the book.

Page after page.

Until that invisible puppeteer made my hand freeze.

I fixed my eyes on the squiggly letters. They scuttled into place to form . . . a *recipe*?

Then with another little shimmy, more words formed at the top of the page: "The Morphology of Morphing."

"Morphing," I breathed. "What's that?"

I read on:

"Of blood, of spirit, one may be,
If this spell one dares to speak.
Drink the potion, tell the plot,
Become one whom you are not!"

I blinked. The squiggly letters didn't move. I blinked harder. Yup, still there.

I still couldn't quite believe my eyes. But my gut was shouting at me, "You can change! You can turn into someone else. You can — *morph*!"

In other words, I could escape!

Chapter Seven

I clutched the book and dashed to the front of the bookmobile. I thrust my library card at Bo the Book Man.

Bo looked me up and down. He peered at the heavy, ancient book in my arms. Then he waved my card away. With a wink, he pointed out the door of the bookmobile.

"Go," he intoned.

I went.

I raced up the long road to my house. My mind was racing, too.

"I could become anyone," I breathed. "I could be Harriet the Spy, sneaking all over New York City! I could be an Indian princess, riding elephants everywhere I go. I could be on TV!"

Before I hid the book in my school bag, I copied down the ingredients for the morphing potion. It included all sorts of odd stuff from around the house, like a bit of rotten cheese from an unused mousetrap and a swatch of hair from an ancestor.

I snuck around the house, gathering scrapings from a cast iron skillet, a cup of lye, some hair from Mamaw's brush and eighteen broom straws.

The whole time, I continued to mutter to myself.

"Who will I be, who will I *be*?"

It was so hard to decide. Chelsea Clinton? Naw — no privacy. An Eskimo chief? Too cold. How about a Parisian pastry chef? A Caribbean deep-sea diver? The choices were all *too* wonderful!

When I got ready for bed that night, I was still mulling things over.

I gazed at the rough log walls of my loft. I looked at my tattered thin quilt. At my taped-up shoes, tossed in the corner. And, in the mirror, at my skinny, sallow cheeks.

Whoever I morphed into, I decided, she was going to be pretty. And well fed! Hmm, maybe a Parisian pastry chef would be a good choice after all...

Then my eyes fell on Mamaw. She had become so weak. Her lips moved feverishly. But, as usual, no sound came out.

Slowly, I tiptoed over to her bed and kissed her furrowed brow. She relaxed a little. I think she even tried to smile.

And that's when I knew. I knew what I had to do. It was going to be the biggest sacrifice of my life!

Chapter Eight

The next day was Sunday.

Some Sundays, we go to church services conducted by Reverend Bluestone, the traveling preacher. The morning is filled with hymns. Then there's Sunday school. *Then* Reverend Bluestone gives a very loud, fire-and-brimstone sermon.

It's a *long* day.

But luckily, Reverend Bluestone was preaching in some other holler today. So all I had to do was listen while Daddy read a few bible passages after breakfast.

Then I was free!

I'd stuffed the magic recipe book and all my morphing ingredients into my book bag. I ran up to the loft to get it from under the bed.

I checked all the contents. The bottle of almond flavoring. The husk from a dead cricket. . . . Yup — I had everything I needed. I slung the heavy bag onto my shoulder.

Then I went to Mamaw's bedside.

I gazed at her face. Her cloudy, blue eyes were filled with sorrow.

"Mamaw," I whispered, "I'm going now. I'm on a mission. I'm going to find our fortune. I'm going to change our destiny! I know you can't understand what I mean. But just hang on, Mamaw. Stay with us! You'll see!"

I tried to wink at her. But all I did was squeeze out a tear. Then I scurried down the stairs.

Mama was ironing in the kitchen while Daddy scanned the Sears Roebuck catalog. I could see Jud out the back window, plowing our land.

"Well," I announced. "I'm leaving. For the day, I mean. Going, uh, fishing! With Sarah. You know, Sarah from school?"

"I know who Sarah is," Mama muttered. She didn't look up from the worn shirt on her ironing board as she said, "Well go on, then. Try to catch us a few catfish for dinner, y'hear?"

"I will," I said shakily. Then, on impulse, I kissed Mama on the cheek. I kissed Daddy too.

"Well," Daddy huffed, embarrassed. "Are you gonna go or aren't you?"

"I'm going," I called.

I went.

Chapter Nine

I ran through the woods next to our house. There was a brambly path through the trees that only I knew about.

It led to my secret hiding place.

Actually, it wasn't a secret. It was the mouth of the old coal mine — condemned, boarded up and overgrown. Everybody knows about it, but I'm the only one who goes there. Some kids at school say it's haunted.

But I've never been scared of this place. I love it.

It's like a cave — a cradle made of cool, red clay. About ten feet in, you hit a wall made of haphazardly nailed boards. Crumbling tin signs are propped against the wall. They read, "Danger. Mine shaft. Condemned. Do not cross."

Behind that wall is a tunnel that leads deep into the dead mine.

When I want to be alone, this is where I go. I take something to eat, a candle and a book.

And this is where I was going to mix my potion and change into . . . I couldn't even think about it.

If I thought too hard, I *knew* it wouldn't work. I just had to plunge in.

So I did.

I laid out my ingredients. I flipped open my dusty book and read the instructions carefully. On the next page, I noticed, were the instructions for morphing back into myself.

"That's funny," I muttered. "The return trip has all these different requirements." I glanced at another long list of ingredients. I sighed.

"I'll just deal with this when the time comes," I decided. "First things first, after all."

Then I commenced to mixing. The book said I had to grind up the dead cricket with the skillet scrapings and rotten cheese. Then I was supposed to whisk the mixture with the broom straws, bind it with the hair and steep it in hot water to make a tea.

Over the flame of my candle, I boiled some water in a tin cup. While I waited, I dabbed my temples and wrists with the almond flavoring. The puzzling, poetic instructions said:

"For remembrance sake,
This scent you'll take."

"I don't get this part," I mused as I rubbed the nutty liquid into my skin. "Not that the rest of this recipe makes any sense, either."

My stomach fluttered as I moved on to the last step.

"Chant the name of who you'll be
Drink the tea and he is thee!"

I took a whiff of the water, with the bundle of bug, hair and rotten cheese still in it. "Ugh!" I cried. "It's disgusting!"

My stomach lurched.

But then I thought of Mamaw's distracted eyes.

And *then* I took a deep breath.

"I will be," I chanted, "my grandmother. My mamaw as a girl. I will solve the mystery of my family's lost fortune. I will change my family's fate!"

I said it over and over again: "My mamaw as a girl. I will be my mamaw as a girl."

Then I held my breath. I held my nose. I slammed back the cup of tea in one revolting gulp!

I grunted at the awful taste of it. But I swallowed it all down.

Then I gasped.

I lurched to my feet. I stumbled towards the mouth of the cave. But I couldn't . . . get . . . to . . . it.

The cave was spinning, spinning!

A wave of nausea swept through me. And my throat was closing up!

I wheezed.

I choked!

I fell to my knees. It . . . was . . . getting . . . dark.

Blackness!

Chapter Ten

I was staring at the roof of the cave. Blinking. Slowly. My eyelids felt heavy. My whole *body* felt heavy.

"What . . . happened?" I groaned.

Like an evening fog, the memory came to me. I had made the tea. I had drunk the potion. Then I must have passed out.

Weakly, I turned my head towards the mouth of the cave. It was still sunny. Maybe I hadn't been out that long.

Slowly, I turned my head to the other side. Then I gasped!

"Wh-where's th-th-the wall?" I stuttered.

The entire wall — at least ten feet of boards and nails — had disappeared into thin air! I was staring into a long dark tunnel.

I struggled to sit up. I heard a sound! It was coming from the tunnel. It sounded like somebody whistling!

And then, deep in the darkness, I saw a pin-point of light. It was bobbing towards me.

With a surge of strength, I scrambled to my feet and ran to hide in the shadows at the side of the cave. I was almost at the dirt wall when I lurched to a halt.

I was teetering at the edge of a hole in the ground!

It was about a foot and a half wide, with a ladder made of flexible cables running up one side of it. It was so deep I couldn't see the bottom.

I was going to fall in!

I flapped my arms.

I swayed forward.

I swayed backward.

Finally I fell safely on my side, huffing and puffing and staring angrily at a wooden sign: "Emergency Exit. Watch yore step."

"*Now* you tell me," I hissed.

I heard the whistling again. The light was almost here!

I hopped around the emergency exit hole and flattened myself against the wall.

The whistling was replaced by a man's voice! "Well, we made it through another day, eh, Tweety?"

The man stepped out of the tunnel's inky darkness and sucked in the fresh air.

He was so strangely dressed!

Underneath a layer of black coal dust, he wore baggy trousers held up by suspenders. His hair was parted in the middle and slicked down. And his mustache! It was waxy and long and it stuck off of either side of his lip like a handlebar.

In one hand, the man held an old-fashioned

lantern. In the other, he held a cage with a little yellow canary inside.

He was peering into the cage and chatting with the bird. I suppressed a giggle as he walked down a dirt road away from the mine.

Then it hit me!

There *was* no dirt road leading up to the mine! There were only trees outside of my cave.

I gulped.

I looked down.

My jeans and T-shirt had disappeared. My duct-taped sneakers were gone!

My legs, which looked a little plumper than usual, were sticking out of a flowery dress with a dropped waist. On my feet? High-ankled brown leather boots!

The ends of my hair were no longer blond. They were brown! And corkscrewed! And tied with shiny ribbons.

I gasped. Mamaw's hair used to be brown! I gaped at the working mineshaft. I flashed to the man with the old-timey hairdo.

I had traveled back in time!

I'd become my grandmother as a twelve-year-old girl!

I whispered, "*I have morphed!*"

Chapter Eleven

I dashed out of the cave and ran down the dirt road. I hopped over a strange mini-train track with some big carts of coal on it.

The trees looked different, too. Kind of gray.

I touched one and my finger came away smudged with black. Coal dust!

Even with the unfamiliar road — not to mention the unfamiliar shoes, which kept making me trip — it wasn't hard to find my way home. After all, I've known every inch of Bearhead Holler since I could walk.

But when I saw my house, I almost didn't recognize it! I skidded to a stop. I felt my new corkscrewy hair bounce around my ears.

My house was lovely! It looked almost new!

I slapped my forehead. What was I thinking? It *was* almost new. Mamaw's parents had built the house as newlyweds.

It had a shiny tin roof, a front porch that didn't sag and an outhouse out back that wasn't rickety.

The house also looked, well, more like a home than it did in 1999.

Clay pots of flowers sat all along the porch

29

rail. On the porch's long picnic table, I saw a bowl brimming with red and yellow apples.

A brown-haired, plump lady in a long dress stood by the front door. She was churning butter.

She saw me!

She waved and shouted, "Betty Marie, where *have* you been, girl? You have a *lot* of work to do here!"

I stared at her dumbly. I looked behind me. Nobody else was there.

"Betty!" the lady scowled. "Have you gone deef?"

Deef? Betty?

Suddenly I jumped! Mamaw's name was Betty Marie. Which meant that lady was my great-grandmother! Whom I'd never met before. I stared at her with my mouth hanging open.

"What is wrong with you?" my great-grandma yelled. "Don't make me come down there and take a switch to you!"

"Oh!" I started running towards the house. "Yes, um, Mama," I called.

With a gulp, I headed inside after this strange woman who, for the time being, was my mother!

Chapter Twelve

Great-grandma immediately put me to work in the cozy, old-fashioned house. As I explored, I found a bank calendar that said 1920!

The loft was still my bedroom. And I recognized some of the sturdy rockers that we still had in 1999.

But everything else was different.

Bright rag rugs covered almost every part of the splintery floor. All the bowls and dishes in the kitchen were of pretty homemade pottery.

There was no refrigerator. After all, you couldn't have a refrigerator with no electricity! Great-grandma sent me out into the woods with the new butter sealed in a crock. I discovered that she kept food cold in the creek, floating it in the water inside a little house called the springhouse.

Wow!

On my way back from the springhouse, I met my great-granddaddy — a serious, almost scary, bearded man who seemed to spend all his time stooped over his plow in the fields.

The stove was a black wood-burning hulk. Pretty soon, I was sweating over it, helping Great-grandma make bread and cakes and pies — when I wasn't dusting, sweeping, polishing or washing!

"So this was what life was like in 1920," I muttered. "They don't call 'em 'hard times' for nothing."

As I pulled a steaming pie from the oven and set it on the windowsill to cool, I said, "Can I ask, Great-, I mean, Mama, what all this fuss is about?"

My great-grandma wiped the sweat off her brow and planted her fists on her plump hips.

"Why, you *know* what, missy!" she declared. "Our guests are coming from Lexington tomorrow. Those important land surveyors who are going to help us with our new discovery."

Land surveyors! New discovery! I made a little squeak of excitement. Maybe, I thought to myself, these visitors would offer a clue to the mysterious fortune.

Great-grandma continued, "Now I hope you haven't gone and told anybody about our guests, after I directly ordered you not to."

"Oh no, Mama!" I assured her. "How could I have? As you can see, I'd forgotten myself."

I laughed nervously.

Great-grandma squinted at me.

"Something wrong with you, girl?" she asked. "You've been acting queer all afternoon. You know what you need? More to do!"

"What?" I gasped. I had worked harder today than I had in my whole life!

"You think too much, that's your problem," Great-grandma declared. "Idle hands are the work of the devil. Here!"

Into my trembling hands, Great-grandma thrust a hatchet.

"Uh, what's this for — firewood?" I quavered.

"Firewood! Girl, what's come over you?" Great-grandma barked. "No, my dear. That is for tomorrow's main course. I'm putting you in charge of it!"

She pointed out the back window. I peered past her finger. I saw a crowd of hens scratching and pecking in the dirt. I gulped.

"Y-you don't mean . . . " I whispered.

"Oh, yes I do!" Great-grandma cackled. She leaned over and thrust her grinning face into mine. "Go on. Kill us a nice fat one!"

Chapter Thirteen

The next morning, Great-grandma stood in the kitchen holding a milk pail. She pointed me to the cow barn.

"Get to work, lazybones," she ordered. "Your father's already been out in the fields for two hours!"

My shoulders sagged. As I trudged to the back door, my eye fell on the calendar. It was a Monday.

"Hey," I said hopefully. "You know it's Monday, Mama! Shouldn't I be on my way to school?"

"School?" Great-grandma sputtered. "Why I do believe you are tetched in the head! You finished sixth grade in the spring, girl! There is no more school for you. You're done!"

My mouth dropped open. Poor Mamaw! Uh, make that poor *me*!

And good morning cows.

I trudged to my first chore of the day.

After I had milked the cows, Great-grandma put me to work setting out a huge lunch for the land surveyors. A lunch that included — ewww — fresh fried chicken.

Finally, everything was in place. I actually had a minute to breathe. I glanced around the living room.

I wonder if there's a good book here I could read, I mused.

Then I froze!

The book! The book with the morphing potion recipe! Where was it?

I flashed back to the mine. I squeezed my eyes shut and pictured the scene. No, I was sure the book hadn't been there. Which must mean it hadn't traveled back in time with me!

That also meant I had no idea how to morph back into my present-day self!

I started to shake. What was I going to do? Would I be trapped here, cooking and cleaning and killing chickens forever?

I had to find that book!

Then I remembered the copyright date — 1916. And this was 1920. That meant the book was published just four years ago. Surely I could track it down somewhere! Somehow!

I scanned the walls for a clock and spied our old, broken cuckoo clock. Now, of course, it looked almost new, and it worked!

"Wow," I whispered, as the clock struck half-past and little mechanical birds popped out and chirped.

It was 11:30. The surveyors — and maybe the secret of my family's fortune — would arrive in fifteen minutes.

I would just have to worry about my future granddaughter, Amy Fay Jones, later.

35

Chapter Fourteen

A sharp knock rattled the front door. It was the surveyors!

I ran to answer it.

I opened the door to two men. They were both tall — one skinny and the other roly-poly. They were elegantly dressed.

The skinny one removed his hat and pressed it to his chest, covering a vest with shiny buttons and a gold watch chain.

"Ah, little girl," he said, smoothing his pointy waxed mustache with a gloved finger. "Fetch us your mother, won't you? I am Mr. Spindler and this is my associate, Mr. Ratzman."

The other man's face was oily with sweat. He twitched his nose at me. Then he took off *his* hat and thrust it into my hands. He lumbered past me as if I was no more than a servant.

"Mrs. Jones?" He called. "Yoo-hoo, Mrs. Jones!"

Rude!

I hated the land surveyors at once.

Great-grandma rushed out of the back bedroom. She smoothed her hair, untied her apron and offered her hand to the men.

Suddenly, Spindler and Ratzman transformed! They had been bossy as could be to me. But when they saw Great-grandma, they turned sweet as syrup.

Hmph, I thought to myself. Kids sure don't get a lot of respect around here.

"Betty!" Great-grandma's voice was sharp. "Now why haven't you fetched these nice men some lemonade yet?"

See? But all I said was, "Yes, Mama."

For the next half-hour, the surveyors devoured our food like it was their first meal in a week. I stayed on my feet, constantly fetching them *more* potatoes, *more* peach preserves, *more* coffee.

Finally — after Ratzman had stuffed three slices of apple pie into his greasy, little mouth — he spoke.

"So Mrs. Jones, I believe you have something to show us?"

"Oh yes," Great-grandma said. She seemed nervous. "Shall I call my husband in from the acre-age?"

"Of course you needn't," Mr. Spindler said, smirking. "You seem a bright little lady. You can handle this yourself."

Great-grandma giggled and turned beet red. Why didn't she see through Spindler's slimy flattery? I was more suspicious than ever.

"Well, all right then," Grandma said. She went

into the pantry and came out with a flour canister.

She reached in and pulled out a little bundle, wrapped in a dishtowel.

She plunked the bundle onto the kitchen table.

I leaned forward anxiously.

The land surveyors leaned forward anxiously.

Corner by corner, Great-grandma unwrapped the lump. With one last flick of her wrist, it was revealed.

I cried out in surprise!

Chapter Fifteen

"That's it?" I squawked. "A lump of coal?"

But the surveyors were aheming and making pleased-sounding grunts.

"Ah, *coal*! Excellent, Mrs. Jones," Spindler said.

"Quite right," Ratzman agreed, reaching for the lump with squat fingers. His nose twitched back and forth. "Pure. Black. Mmm, yes, very good. Now you say your husband happened upon this coal in his cornfield? And you had no idea it was there?"

"Uh, yessir," Great-grandma said nervously. "We don't know how much of it there is, either."

"Well, that's what we're here to find out," Spindler assured her. "You could make a nice little nest egg if there are several acres."

But Great-grandma didn't seem excited. In fact, she was squirming.

"Oh, you gentlemen are so kind," she cried. "I cain't deceive you!"

She ran to the pantry and pulled out another toweled lump. She thrust it into Spindler's hands. "You see?" Great-grandma said. "It's not *all* pure and black. This chunk seems contaminated. It's shot through with ugly, light rock, see?"

Then she sighed and said lamely, "I'll make you some more coffee while you examine it." She disappeared into the kitchen.

I peered over Spindler's shoulder at the lump in his hand. Great-grandma was right. The black coal was mottled with blobs of whitish-gray rock.

But even more interesting was Spindler's reaction. He gripped the coal with trembling fingers. He gaped at Ratzman. His eyebrows danced and his lips quivered.

Meanwhile, Ratzman's nose was twitching so hard I thought he was going to have a sneezing fit.

"Spindler," he whispered. "Do you know what this means?"

But Spindler coughed loudly. "The girl, the girl!" he hissed.

Clearly Ratzman had forgotten I was there. He turned and glared at me. I smiled sweetly and tried to look innocent.

"Would you like more dessert, Mr. Ratzman?" I cooed, shoving a plate of gingerbread at him.

He started to snarl at me. But he was interrupted by Great-grandma's return.

The men harrumphed and composed themselves. Spindler turned coy and cool.

"Well, Mrs. Jones, unfortunately, you were right," he announced. "This defect in the coal seam could devalue your mineral rights — that is, what we could pay for your coal. Yes, it could take down the price *quite* a bit."

"But we'll have to survey the land to be sure," Ratzman added, examining his fingernails casually.

"Quite right," Spindler said, leaping to his feet. He grabbed the grayish coal chunk and slid it into his pocket. Then he rushed to the door.

"Tell your husband to stay out of his corn field tomorrow," he ordered. "We'll be back then. Good day, madam!"

Then Spindler and Ratzman hurried out the door.

"Well, I do believe we've disappointed them," Great-grandma said sadly.

Suddenly, I noticed something fishy. In their rush to leave, the surveyors had forgotten the other chunk of coal — the nice, pure black one! I grabbed it and ran after them.

"Hey misters!" I called. I caught up to them as the raced down the hill. "You forgot . . . "

Spindler spun around. His eyes were narrowed. His yellow teeth were bared.

"*What do you want, you whippersnapper?*" he growled,

"I j-j-just wanted to give you this," I said, shoving the coal lump at him. "You forgot it!"

Ratzman swiped the coal from my hands. "Thank you my dear," he hissed.

"Thanks for nothin'" Spindler spat. "You'd do best to mind your own business, *little girl*."

41

Chapter Sixteen

I was trembling. I climbed back onto the front porch. Something was very fishy.

Great-grandma poked her head out of the screen door.

"Betty Marie, you have dishes to wash in here!"

"Yes Mama," I said. But I continued to stare at the surveyors as they picked their way down the rocky path. Great-grandma joined me on the porch.

"They sure are in a hurry, aren't they?" I said.

"Well, they're boarding with the Widder Hayes," she replied. "And you know she lives way yonder down the holler. They probably want to get back quick and take a nap after that big meal."

"Uh-huh," I said. But my mind was racing. Those guys were up to something. I had to find out what.

I had to get away!

"Mama," I blurted. "I just remembered, I promised I'd loan some embroidery thread to, to . . ."

Quick, what was a good, old-fashioned name?

"Ethel! Yeah, Ethel," I cried. "She told me yesterday that she was plum out of red and desperately needed some. I *promised* I'd bring it to her."

I held my breath. Please let Mamaw have a friend named Ethel.

"Well, which Ethel, Betty?" Mama said impatiently. "Ethel O'Mears or Ethel Puckett?"

I sighed with relief. "Um, Puckett," I said.

"Well she's our nearest neighbor," Great-grandma said. "She's just down the road a piece. You can go after you finish the dishes."

Oh, no! It would be too late to follow the surveyors by then!

"Did I say Puckett?" I said, slapping my forehead. "I meant Ethel O'Mears!"

"Oh, well, she's right far down the holler," Great-grandma scolded. "You'd better git, girl, if you want to be back by dark. I'll tan your hide if I have to send your daddy out looking for you!"

"OK, Mama!" I cried.

Then I ran!

Chapter Seventeen

Luckily for me, Spindler and Ratzman didn't know our rough mountain roads like I did. It was a cinch to catch up with them as they stumbled down into the holler.

When I had them in sight, I started ducking behind trees and bushes to spy on them.

They were giggling and hopping about. Spindler kept punching Ratzman's arm and yelling, "Son of a gun!"

"Hmmm," I whispered. "What's he so excited about?"

I followed them to a big, rambling house, which must have been the Widow Hayes' place. They went inside. I hid in a pack of bushes nearby, and waited.

And waited.

And waited!

Dusk was falling fast. Great-grandma's going to take a switch to me if I don't start home right now, I thought.

I was just getting ready to leave when the smarmy surveyors emerged from the house.

They were carrying picks and shovels, cloth

bags and what looked like measuring equipment. They started walking back up the holler. Back towards my house!

I slunk along behind them. I followed them up the darkening road. They made a wide circle around my house and crept into Great-granddaddy's cornfield.

Then, while I hid behind a tree nearby, they started digging. They began chipping away chunks of coal that seemed to be right below the surface!

Ratzman held his lantern up to a piece of the coal. "Uh huh! Yup!" he crowed, jumping in place. "There's a ton of it!"

"Hoowee, these hillbillies are dumb!" Spindler said. "Imagine, having no idea that your little shack is sitting on acres and acres of coal — not to mention diamonds! Hooo, we'll be richer than the Rockefellers when we bilk them out of this land!"

Diamonds?

I was so shocked, I fell backwards into some bushes.

"Who's there?" Spindler hissed. He and Ratzman began inching towards my tree.

I squinched my eyes shut. I pressed against the tree trunk. I tried to become invisible.

But my eyes flew open when I heard the next sound: the cocking of a pistol!

Chapter Eighteen

The evil land surveyors — make that *speculators* — were only a few yards away from the tree where I was cringing.

I had nowhere to go.

I was dead meat!

I dropped to the ground, preparing for Spindler's attack.

That's when I saw it. A hole! It looked like the den of an animal — probably a fox. It must have been a fat fox because this hole was pretty wide. Just wide enough . . .

Without a second thought, I jumped in, feet first.

Luckily for me, the hole turned out to be a tunnel — a pretty deep one. I'd just pulled my head into the shadows when I glimpsed the shiny, black shoes of Spindler and Ratzman scratching around the tree.

"Who's there?" Ratzman barked. "Show yourself."

There was a long silence. I held my breath. I heard the men walking around, knocking branches out of their way and swearing.

"Must have just been a deer or something," Spindler sighed. They walked away.

I was shaking. That was a close one!

I could hear the men talking as they finished their shoveling. "So, we should come up with a plan for this deal, eh?" Ratzman said.

"Why bother?" crowed Spindler. "I've dealt with these holler simpletons before. They're so glad for a little cash, it takes almost nothing to get them to sign away their mineral rights. And after the papers are signed — well, it's not our fault if diamonds are discovered, is it?"

They erupted in evil cackles.

I was disgusted. But as I heard the men leave, I grew elated!

I knew the speculators' entire scheme!

All I had to do was tell my great-grandparents! They'd put an end to the deal, of course. Then they would mine the diamonds themselves. Our family would be set forever.

In fact, we'd be more than set.

We'd be rich!

Chapter Nineteen

"Pshaw!" snorted my great-granddaddy.

We were sitting at the kitchen table the next morning. Even though I didn't get to eat breakfast (my punishment for coming home so late the night before) I stayed at the table to tell Mamaw's parents about the speculators' scheme.

They didn't believe me!

"It's true," I protested. "Those knobby rocks in the coal — those are diamonds. Who *knows* how much they're worth!"

"Diamonds!" laughed Great-grandma. "Nonsense. A diamond is sparkly."

"Don't you see?" I cried. "I *heard* Spindler and Ratzman talking about it. They . . . "

"Enough!" Great-granddaddy roared. "I will not have my daughter telling me my business. Children should be seen and not heard!"

He jumped up from the table and stalked out to the front porch.

Then I heard him call, "Ah, good morning Mr. Spindler. Mr. Ratzman. We didn't expect you this early! Betty Marie — get these gentlemen some coffee."

I kicked the table leg angrily. Then I trudged over to the stove to obey.

The men stood outside, chatting with great-granddaddy and slurping up their coffee. Then the three of them trekked out to the cornfield to "survey." As if Spindler and Ratzman didn't already know exactly what lay beneath the cornstalks.

An hour later, they returned. They sat down at the kitchen table. Great-grandma rushed to pour them glasses of iced tea. I stood in the corner of the kitchen and scowled.

"Well," Spindler said, pasting a fake, sorrowful look on his face. "We've decided that we will do you the favor of taking those mineral rights off your hands. But with this impure coal you've got here, we won't be able to pay much."

"Oh," Great-grandma said, sitting down heavily. "Oh, how disappointing. Well, maybe it would be best not to sell. Maybe we'd do better just to keep farming the land."

"*No!*" cried Ratzman. "You can't do that!"

"What?" asked Great-granddaddy.

Spindler cut in, glaring at the pudgy Ratzman.

"What my colleague *means* is, this land won't be farmable for much longer. You see how close the coal is to the surface? That's called erosion of the soil. Once that soil's gone down another few inches, not a seed will grow."

He shook his head sadly and slapped a hand on Great-granddaddy's shoulder. "I'm afraid this is your best option, Mr. Jones."

I couldn't stand it. I was watching the family fortune slip away. This was the very reason I'd morphed into Mamaw. I had to act!

"You know what I heard?" I called from my corner. Every head in the room swiveled towards me. "I heard they found gemstones over there in Camp Creek Holler. The folks who own the land — well, they just built themselves a mansion!"

"You don't say," growled Spindler, glaring at me.

"Yup!" I lied. "I wonder if we've got any of those on our land. Maybe we should check, huh Daddy?"

Ratzman began to sputter a protest. But Great-granddaddy cut him off.

"I apologize for my daughter," he barked. He turned hurt and angry eyes on me.

"Betty Marie, now you stay out of this," he growled. "I know my own business."

Then he thrust his hand out to Spindler. "Sir," he announced, "you've got yourself a deal!"

Chapter Twenty

"Wonderful," exclaimed Spindler. He jumped to his feet and pumped Great-granddaddy's hand. "We'll just take the train back to Lexington and have our lawyer draw up the papers. Let's see, today's Tuesday. We can be back first thing Thursday for you to sign on the dotted line. Sir — you won't be sorry."

He and Ratzman bustled out the door so fast they overturned a glass of tea. They didn't even pause to apologize.

Rude!

I crept to the front door and peeked out at the speculators. They'd paused on the porch to adjust their fancy hats and gloves.

"Hee hee, we did it," Ratzman whispered.

"Yes, despite the efforts of that smarty pants hillbilly girl," Spindler hissed. "You know, she could make trouble for us."

Absent-mindedly, he polished his gold pocket watch. "Hey," he said, "Don't you know a fella around here? A Clem Greeley?"

"Oh, yeah," Ratzman replied. "Big brute of a guy. Mean one."

"Quite," Spindler said dryly. "You know, he could shut up our little nuisance nicely, couldn't he?"

I froze in terror.

"Yes, that's it," Spindler said. "Let's go find him right now. You know, there are mine shafts all over these mountains. A little thing like her — she's liable to fall right in!"

Chapter Twenty-One

I was sitting on the porch steps, wringing my hands. What was I going to do?

Suddenly, I spied a small, wiry girl who looked about my age. She was tromping up the road to my house.

"Hi there," she called. She waved at me eagerly.

"Uh, hello," I said.

She stopped at my feet. She cocked her head to the side. She wrinkled her freckled nose. Her blond hair, which was straight as a stick, was cut in a short bob.

"Well," the girl said, planting her feet apart. "You're sure being stand-offish this morning."

"Oh," I said, giggling nervously. "I'm always that way with people I've just met. Don't worry, I'll warm up."

"Just met?" The girl cocked her head to the other side. "Why Betty Marie Jones, I'm only Ethel Puckett, your nearest neighbor and best girlfriend since you were two! Why I declare, I'm hurt by your malfeasance!"

Ethel Puckett! One of the Ethels I'd lied to

Great-grandma about.

"Oh, *Ethel*!" I exclaimed. "Ethel Puckett! Of course!"

"What's wrong with you?" Ethel asked. "You don't seem yourself. You're all discombobulated."

Before I had a chance to answer, she chattered on. "How do you like that? I've used *two* extra-long words. Malfeasance and discombobulated. You dared me to learn a big new word every day and I am doing it! I'll show *you*."

"Uh, right," I said, trying to laugh with her. But all I could do was sigh.

"OK, out with it," Ethel said, punching me in the arm.

"What's wrong?" she continued. "You've got that look that you always get when you want to tell something but you're being stubborn about it."

I knew exactly what look she was talking about. I'd seen it about a million times on Mamaw's face. Now, of course, it was on *my* face.

I gulped. Well, the grown-ups hadn't believed me. Maybe Ethel would.

So I told her everything about the speculators, my spying and the lode of diamonds in my daddy's cornfield.

I did *not*, of course, tell Ethel about my morphing. *Nobody* would believe that!

When I finished the story, Ethel's mouth was frozen in a big, wide O.

"Oh, my," she breathed. "Diamonds in the corn

field. Golly, who'da thunk?"

"Sooo," I said impatiently, "You got any ideas?"

"Nope!" Ethel said cheerfully. "Let me see a chunk of that coal with the diamonds in it!"

"I don't have any," I wailed. "The speculators took the samples they dug up. And we can't get into the field because Great-, uh, I mean, Daddy's out there harvesting before the dig. And he's mad at me already."

"Well I don't foresee us proving anything without the evidence, do you?" Ethel said. "We've got to get a hunk of that coal."

"But Daddy will be in the field all day," I lamented. "And we only have two days!"

"Well, after you stop your bellyaching," Ethel said, rolling her eyes, "how 'bout we check the fox tunnels?"

"You know about that fox tunnel by that big oak tree?" I asked.

"Tun-*nels*! And excuse me, but we've been crawling around in those since we were in kindygarten," Ethel blurted. "Lord, your memory's slight today. Don't you remember that summer I was grounded for walking the ridgepole of the roof? And we dug into all those foxholes so I could sneak out and play with you? We must have dug a mile of tunnels down there. I bet they're still good!"

"Well, at least *one* of them is," I remembered with a shudder. "One right by the cornfield! Let's go!"

Chapter Twenty-Two

We stopped at Great-grandpa's shed for picks and a lantern. Then we snuck around the outskirts of the cornfield, where Great-grandpa was hard at work.

Finally, we made it to the big oak tree. There was the foxhole.

"Whoo hoo," Ethel whistled softly, peering into the hole. "This does take me back!"

Then she punched me in the arm again. Ow! What was this, some sort of secret handshake? Before I had a chance to return the gesture, Ethel grabbed the lantern and dove, head first, into the tunnel.

"Ethel?" I called shakily. "Uh, how's it going in there?"

Her voice was muffled. "Why don't you come in and see, scaredy cat!"

I sighed and grabbed our tools. Then I crawled in behind Ethel.

We inched along like moles. We scratched away clumps of dirt and plant roots. I couldn't see much of anything except Ethel's high-ankled boots skittering ahead of me.

But oh, I could hear her!

"Well, looky there, a toad just hit me in the

nose," she called. "You OK back there? Hope my feet don't stink! Hee hee!"

I rolled my eyes and called, "Keep crawling Ethel! Do you see any coal?"

She gasped. "I think this might be coal right here in front of me. Except it's got these knobby, white rocks in it!"

"Those are the diamonds," I yelled. I passed a pick up towards Ethel's right arm. "Grab a chunk and we can get out of here!"

"OK," she called. "I'm reaching, I'm reeeachiiing . . ."

I heard a strange rumble. Then I heard a muffled squeal: "Betty? Betty! Help me!"

"Ethel, what happened?" I screeched.

"Cave-in. While I was reaching my arms out. My arms — they're trapped. I can't move 'em. And the dirt's right against my face, Betty! I only have about an inch of air to breathe! I'm scared!"

I backed up a little and started yanking on Ethel's boots. But all that budged were the boots. They came right off in my hands.

"You're wedged in," I yelled. "I'll go get Daddy!"

"No!" Ethel called. "He'll tan our hides good if he finds out we came down here! You'll have to go around — use the tunnel that bumps into this one up ahead. Remember? You can dig me out from the other side. You remember, don't ya, Betty?"

I was in a panic! How could I tell Ethel that of

57

course I didn't remember? That I wasn't even really Betty Marie Jones!

I tuned out Ethel's voice.

I squeezed my eyes shut.

Think like Mamaw, I said to myself.

Then, through a haze in my head, a picture came to me. It was faint and fuzzy.

But it got clearer.

And clearer.

It was a maze of tunnels. I knew where to go!

I scrunched forward and grabbed the lantern. I patted Ethel on the shoulder. "Keep calling my name," I said. "Don't stop, whatever you do!"

I started scuffling back through the tunnel. I passed the hole where we'd dropped in and kept going.

And then I saw it! A passage jutting off to the left, just as I'd seen it in my mind.

I dove into the tunnel. I started crawling as fast as I could. As I crawled, I strained my ears.

I couldn't hear a thing!

"Ethel," I yelled, "are you there? Call my name!"

Nothing!

I crawled further, scrambling and scraping and bumping the dirt walls with my face.

"Ethel?" I screamed.

Chapter Twenty-Three

"Betty?"

What was that? It sounded like a tiny chipmunk, squeaking.

I crawled forward a little. "Ethel, where are you?" I yelled.

"Betty."

I turned to my left and started pawing frantically at the dirt. I dug and dug. I yelped in pain as one of my fingernails tore.

Then I struck an arm!

Ethel's arm!

"Eeek," I heard, "something's got me!"

"*I've* got you," I screamed. I kept digging until I reached her. We clutched each other.

"It's a miracle," Ethel breathed dramatically. "Thank you Betty! You have emancipated me from certain death!"

"Nice vocabulary," I said. Then I grabbed the pick and chinked off a lump of the white-flecked coal.

"OK, let's get out of here," I said.

We went!

Finally, we crawled out of the foxhole. We were so muddy and dirty, I wouldn't have recognized my face — make that Mamaw's face — if I looked in the mirror.

As Ethel and I brushed ourselves off, I noticed a big, hairy hulk of a man.

He was leaning against a birch tree a few yards away. He had a barrel chest, a scraggly beard and beady little eyes that glared out from under one long, black, bushy eyebrow.

He was squinting at us and chewing on a piece of grass.

"Ewww, who's that," I whispered.

"Oh, you know, that's just Clem Greeley," Ethel said.

"Oh," I said.

Then I froze. Clem Greeley?

I pictured the smarmy Mr. Spindler saying, "Don't you know a fella around here? A Clem Greeley? He could shut up our little nuisance nicely, couldn't he?"

I gasped.

Then I grabbed Ethel's hand.

"*Ruuun!*" I screamed.

Chapter Twenty-Four

Ethel and I raced through the woods down the holler. I could hear the rasping breaths of Clem as he clomped along right behind us.

"I don't . . . know . . . why . . . you . . . girlies . . . even . . . bother," he yelled out between huffs and puffs. "I'm much . . . bigger . . . than . . . you . . . I'm only . . . gonna . . . catch ya!"

"Oh yeah?" I shouted. I followed Ethel as she hopped over a fallen tree trunk. "You know what they say, 'The bigger they are, the harder they fall!'"

"We'll see about that!" Clem grunted. Then he leapt through the air. He was headed straight for me!

"*Aaaaah*," I shrieked.

In mid-air, Clem grabbed one of my corkscrew curls.

We both fell to the ground — me with a small thump and Clem with a huge thud.

"*Ooof*," he grunted. The breath was knocked out of him. I helped matters by aiming one of my hard-soled boots right for his heaving stomach.

"*Argh!*" he yelled, dropping my hair to clutch at his middle.

"Ha!" I shouted. I jumped to my feet and dashed off.

Ethel was way ahead of me. "This way," she shouted, veering to the left. "To Mr. Roper's dairy farm!"

"Whatever you say," I yelled, racing after her. I guess Clem had recovered. I could hear his big feet crashing through the brush behind me.

"Ethel, he's catching up again," I called.

"Trust me," she screamed. She'd come to a split rail fence! What now?

Ethel made a sharp right and began running alongside the fence. Bewildered, I followed.

"Ethel," I cried. "Let's hop the fence!"

"Not yet," she ordered.

"Why not?" I huffed. By now, I could almost feel Clem's breath on the back of my neck!

"You'll see," Ethel shouted over her shoulder.

So we ran.

And ran.

We followed that split rail fence forever, it seemed.

Finally, Ethel screeched to a halt.

"Now!" she yelled. "Betty, jump long and far!"

I watched as she scrambled over the rails and leaped way out into the meadow. Five seconds later, I was lying in the grass next to her.

"Peee-eeew! What's that smell?" I blurted.

Then I forgot the stench completely! I pointed and screamed!

"*Clemmmm!*"

Chapter Twenty-Five

Clem Greeley had not been deterred. Though he was sweating buckets and wheezing badly, he began to lumber over the fence.

But he was too big and clumsy to jump out into the meadow the way Ethel and I had. He merely rolled over the top rail with a grunt and a plop.

A loud plop.

A smelly plop.

"Aaaargh," Clem shouted in disgust.

Ethel started shrieking with laughter. "Ha, ha! The biggest dung heap in Bearhead Holler and Clem is making himself comfortable right in it!"

I joined in the joke. "Whoo hoo! Fee, Fi, Fo, Fum, I'm Clem Greeley and I'm real dumb!"

Clem shook his fist at us, but he was too exhausted and encrusted with cow manure to chase us. Ethel and I ran off, skipping and laughing.

"I'm gonna git you!" Clem called.

Chapter Twenty-Six

We ran and hid in Ethel's daddy's barn.

I flung myself onto a hay bale. Ethel skipped over to say hello to a sleepy-eyed brown horse. She held our coal chunk up to his nose.

"Do those little rocks look like diamonds to you?" Ethel asked the horse. It snorted.

"Me either," Ethel responded.

"That's the problem," I moaned. "Who could believe those little knobs are raw diamonds? None of the poor folk around here could possibly know what raw diamonds look like."

"So what we need is someone smart and rich," Ethel declared. "Someone with experience with this sort of thing."

"Where on earth would we find someone like that in Bearhead Holler?" I wailed.

Ethel gasped. She jumped onto my hay bale and shook me by the shoulders. "I've got it! Miss Montgomery!"

"M-m-miss Wh-who?" I stuttered as Ethel jangled me about.

"*You* know, the schoolteacher," Ethel said.

I thought about the teachers at my school back

home. I mean, in the present. Most of them were underpaid. And frazzled. And, well, just smart enough to get quickie teaching certificates from the community college.

"Are you sure some schoolteacher is the best person to go to?" I quavered.

"Well, Miss Montgomery isn't just any schoolteacher,' Ethel scoffed. "*You* know her story."

"Refresh my memory," I said with a sigh. It was getting tiresome not knowing anything.

"It's a *tragic* tale," Ethel said dreamily. "Miss Montgomery was the daughter of one of the most important men in Lexington. She had it all. She even went to a teaching college in Boston.

"Then she came back to Lexington. She was going to teach history at a fancy girls' academy. But her daddy had other plans. He tried to marry her off to a well-connected man, but he was cruel and twice her age. She ran away to Bearhead Holler and got a job teaching at our little school. And she hasn't seen her family since."

We both sighed.

"Poor Miss Montgomery," I lamented.

Ethel broke out of her reverie. "Oh, things aren't *so* bad for Miss Montgomery," she said brightly. "She is being courted by that cute Mr. Hughes!"

"Do you think she'll want to help us?" I asked.

"'Course!" Ethel announced importantly. "She adores me! She's the one who gave me my dictionary so I can *augment* my *illustrious* vocabulary. Come on. Let's go!"

Chapter Twenty-Seven

Miss Montgomery lived in a simple, one-room cabin at the base of the holler. But when she opened the door, her lipsticked smile seemed to fill the room with glamour.

"Ethel! Betty Marie!" she exclaimed. "What a nice surprise. I was just taking some cinnamon buns out of the oven."

She was beautiful. She had wavy red hair twirled into a bun at the base of her neck. Her skin was as white as china. As she set a plate of steaming sweet rolls on the table, I noticed sparkly rubies bobbing from her earlobes.

"Wow, where did you get those earrings?" I asked.

"I inherited them from my grandmother," Miss Montgomery said sadly. "Before I . . . before I left Lexington. My grandfather had quite an eye for fine gemstones."

"Well actually," Ethel said, "That's why we're here. We need your help. We need a grown-up who can convince Betty's parents that there are raw diamonds in their coal!"

After I explained everything to Miss Montgomery, Ethel plunked our smudgy coal lump on the clean tablecloth.

Rude!

I kicked her under the table.

"Ow!" she cried, glaring at me.

"That's OK, Betty," Miss Montgomery laughed, picking up the coal and whisking the black dust away with her fingers. "Well, this is the most unusual piece of coal I've ever seen."

She examined the lump, turning it this way and that with a frown on her face. Finally, she sighed.

"I just don't know girls," she said. "I've read geology books. They describe raw diamonds found in Africa. And I do know that those diamonds were dull and whitish before they were cut and polished. But I haven't seen a picture. So I can't say I know whether these are diamonds.

"And since I never met these deceitful speculators, I doubt your parents would believe me either, Betty," she said sympathetically. "You know, your parents don't think much of schools, or schoolteachers."

"Yeah," I said, moping.

Miss Montgomery picked up a cinnamon bun and munched thoughtfully. Then she swallowed abruptly and cried, "I don't know why I didn't think of it earlier! Mr. Hicks!"

"Who's that?" Ethel asked.

"A jeweler I used to know in Lexington," Miss Montgomery said. "He was a friend of the family. A very odd man. But a brilliant craftsman when it came to gems. I bet he could identify a raw diamond with one eye covered and one hand tied behind his back."

"Well that'd be great, if he wasn't all the way in Lexington," I said.

"Oh, Lexington is just an inexpensive train ride away," Miss Montgomery said. "I'm sure if you asked your parents, they'd take you there. Surely they'd be open to *talking* with Mr. Hicks."

Coming from Miss Montgomery, that sounded like the most logical idea in the world.

"You're right, Miss Montgomery," I said. "Thank you so much. I'm going to go talk to them at supper tonight."

"Thanks for the cinnamon buns too," Ethel said, snatching a couple of them from the plate before running with me to the door.

"Good luck, girls," the teacher called after us.

Ethel and I raced up the holler road towards my house. When we were almost there, Ethel veered onto a tree-lined drive.

"Where are you going?" I demanded.

"Home!" she said with her mouth full of cinnamon bun. "I left all my chores undone while we were running around. I don't want my mama to get any madder at me than she already is."

"You're not going to help me talk to my parents?" I wailed.

"Heck no!" Ethel said. "You know your daddy always scared me a little bit!"

"Me, too," I whispered.

"Come on," Ethel comforted me. "You know your parents so well. You'll be able to wheedle a trip to Lexington out of them, easy. By tomorrow night, you'll be back triumphant from the big city. And rich too!"

I wanted to yell, "I don't know my parents at all! I'm not Betty Marie! I'm just Amy!"

But all I said was, "Uh, you're probably right. OK, see you tomorrow then."

"Triumphant!" Ethel yelled, raising a fist in the air.

"Uh huh," I quavered.

Then I gulped hard and headed "home."

Chapter Twenty-Eight

"*Lexington*?" Great-granddaddy slammed his knife and fork on the kitchen table so hard the glasses shimmied and the dishes shuddered. "Absolutely not, young lady. I told you to keep out of this!"

"But Daddy, what if those rocks *are* diamonds and not just impure coal?" I asked. "Aren't you curious? We may be rich beyond our wildest dreams."

But Great-grandma and Great-granddaddy wouldn't hear of a trip to the city.

"You're dreaming, girl," Great-granddaddy said. "And I don't need to visit some stranger in the city to see that those ugly rocks aren't diamonds!"

"Isn't it worth the risk . . . " I began. But Great-grandma interrupted.

"*Elizabeth Marie Jones*," she said. "You are disrespecting your parents. You *know* that your father can't work in the mines. He had consumption as a child and his lungs can't take the coal dust. This land is our livelihood. Selling these mineral rights is the only way to keep putting food on the table.

"Now you get to bed and stop talking nonsense about things you don't understand!"

"It's you who doesn't understand," I whispered as I trudged up the steps to the loft.

But I didn't go to sleep.

I didn't even go to bed.

I waited.

And I waited.

Finally, Great-grandma smothered the fire in the big, black stove. Great-granddaddy snuffed out his corn cob pipe. They went to their bedroom and shut the door.

In a flash, I stuffed the chunk of diamond-coal in my skirt pocket. I raced down the loft steps. Silently, I slipped out the front door.

I started running down the road.

I was making a break for it!

Chapter Twenty-Nine

Soon, I was standing in some bushes, throwing pebbles at an upstairs window of Ethel's house.

"Please let this be Ethel's window," I whispered.

Mamaw, of course, would know exactly which window belonged to her best friend. Me — I could only guess.

After a few minutes, Ethel stuck her head out the window. I had been right! Ethel yawned, then mumbled, "Who's there? Is it my secret admirer?"

I couldn't resist. I lowered my voice to a growl and replied, "Oh Ethel, my darling, your face moves me more than a Moon Pie. Your voice, it's like mockingbirds to my ears. I, Clem Greeley, have come to declare my undying devotion."

"Eeeeww!" Ethel screeched. "Clem Greeley!"

I let out a giggle.

"Got you, Juliet," I called. "Now could you kindly get dressed and come down from yonder window? And bring some food. We're going on mission impossible."

"Mission impossible," Ethel repeated. "Catchy.

I'll be right down."

Five minutes later, she emerged wearing a dress and sweater and carrying a small, cloth bag.

"I've got a poke full of leftovers from supper," she offered. "Fried chicken and pecan pie. So what are we doing?"

"Mama and Daddy *refuse* to go to Lexington to find that jeweler," I said. "So I'm going myself! I have no money, so I'll have to sneak on to the train. And Ethel, I need you to go with me. I need your help!"

Ethel started trembling. "I don't know, Betty," she said. "My parents will whup me good if I sneak out."

"Mine too," I said.

"And I've never been on a train before."

"Me either," I said.

It was the truth. I'd only ridden the bus on my few short trips out of the holler.

"But Ethel, trust me," I said. "This is for more than just me and my mama and daddy. It's about much more than that. Oh, if only I could make you understand."

Ethel gripped me by the shoulders. I braced myself for a shake, but she only squeezed. "Betty Marie," she whispered, "you've been my best friend since we were two. I trust you. Besides, like I said, I've never been on a train before!"

That's when I noticed that Ethel's eyes were gleaming. Not with fear, but with excitement.

"Maybe we could eat in the dining car!" I said.

"We'll go to the gaming car and play cards," Ethel squealed.

"We'll sit on red velvet banquettes," I said, jumping up and down.

"What's a banquette?" Ethel asked.

"I don't know, but doesn't it sound wonderful?" I replied.

We giggled and started running down the holler.

Chapter Thirty

By dawn, we had almost reached the train depot.

It was Wednesday morning — a damp, shadowy, foggy morning. We only had until tomorrow to outwit Spindler and Ratzman.

And come to think of it, I hadn't had a minute to try to track down the morphing recipe book!

I shook my head as we walked towards the depot. I couldn't think about that now. First I had to save the fortune. *Then* I'd think about morphing back into myself.

And if I never found the book, well, at least Mamaw's life — uh, *my* life — would be a lot better than it might have been. As good as a life could be, that is, with no modern things, and no bookmobile and no school and . . .

"Betty, what's wrong? You look positively stricken," Ethel said as she tromped along beside me.

"What? Oh, nothing," I said, trying to shake all thoughts of morphing from my head. "I was . . . just wondering how we're going to sneak onto the train, that's all."

Hmmm, let me think," Ethel said. Then she

grabbed my arm excitedly. "Hey, there it is!"

The road ended at a long boardwalk. On one side of the walk was the train station. And on the other — the train!

The engine, which was resting at our end of the walk, was *beautiful*, with red racing stripes running along its sides.

"It's straight out of a history museum!" I gasped.

"What are you talking about?" Ethel laughed. "It looks like the latest thing to me! Hey, I have an idea. Let's walk down to the caboose. We'll circle around to the other side of the train, where nobody can see us. And then we'll jump into a baggage car or something like that!"

"Great plan," I said.

Trying to act casual, we walked quickly down the boardwalk.

It was almost empty.

It was actually kind of eerie.

The fog swirled around our feet. There wasn't a sound except my footsteps. And Ethel's footsteps.

And somebody else's footsteps!

I clutched Ethel's arm. We stopped suddenly.

Just a second too late, the other footsteps stopped too.

We started again.

So did those footsteps.

I whipped around. "Who's there?" I called. "Who's following us?"

A form stepped slowly out of the swirling shadows. It had a barrel chest. And matted black hair. And it smelled of dung.

"Clemmm!" I yelled.

We started racing down the boardwalk. Clem cackled and started loping after us.

But if he was gaining on us, I couldn't hear it. His footsteps — and everything else for that matter — were drowned out by the shriek of the train whistle.

A man's voice rang out: "All aboard!"

"Nooooo," I shouted.

Chapter Thirty-One

Ethel and I dashed down the boardwalk.

But we weren't dodging trees in the woods or hopping fences now. Clem was gaining on us fast!

I glanced over my shoulder to get a glimpse of him. I tripped and tumbled to the boardwalk!

Clem leapt on me before I could even scream!

Pinning my legs to the ground with one meaty knee, he reached for my waist. He was going to carry me off and throw me into a mineshaft!

"Ethel, help me!" I cried.

Ethel scanned the ground. She hopped off the boardwalk and, out of the gravel next to the railroad tracks, she fished a huge, heavy railroad spike. It was almost a foot long. Its head was two inches across.

Gripping the spike by the pointy end, Ethel bounded over to me and Clem. She raised her arm over her head.

"Make sure you don't hit me!" I screeched.

That made Ethel hesitate. At the same moment, Clem whirled around.

And lunged straight for Ethel!

Chapter Thirty-Two

"*Aiyeeee!*" Ethel screamed. In her terror, she flung the spike out of her hand.

And wouldn't you know, it bashed Clem right in the forehead!

"Ugh," he gurgled. He fell to his knees. He wobbled a bit. Then he passed out.

"Yes!" Ethel called. She reached down to help me to my feet. "We did it!"

"Not quite," I yelled. "The train's leaving!"

While we'd been fighting off Clem, the train had started to chug out of the depot.

Ethel and I started racing alongside the train. I spotted an empty cattle car, with an open door.

Without pausing to think, I leapt through the air. The top half of my body landed in the car. With a lot of kicking and struggling, I pulled the rest of myself in.

Where was Ethel?

I turned around and screamed!

Ethel was running alongside the train. She was struggling to keep up.

And Clem was waking up!

He lurched to his feet. He shook his head. He

gaped at the departing train. Then he started to bound after Ethel.

"Betty, he's gonna git me!" she screamed

"Not if you jump!" I shouted. "Ethel — trust me. I'll catch you!"

I braced myself and held my hands out.

She jumped and caught my hands!

"Pull, Betty!" she shrieked. "Pull me in!"

I pulled. I yanked. And I tugged.

Ethel's boots were hitting the railroad ties with a *thump, thump, thump.*

"Ow. Ow! Ow!" she yelled.

Clem galloped along the boardwalk. He was gaining on her! Then he leapt through the air to grab her.

I gritted my teeth and gave a tremendous yank.

Ethel tumbled into the cattle car.

And Clem tumbled to the ground!

He'd never catch up now. The train began to pick up speed. We were on our way to the big city and the jeweler, Mr. Hicks.

And the key to my family's fortune!

Chapter Thirty-Three

A few hours later, the train chugged into Lexington.

Ethel and I rolled stiffly out of the cattle car onto a boardwalk just like the one at the Bearhead Holler depot. We picked hay out of our hair.

"So much for the dining car," Ethel said glumly. We had eaten our sack lunch sitting on a hay bale.

"Yeah. And the red velvet banquettes," I said.

We walked into the big, fancy train station.

"Wow!" Ethel and I said together. Inside the station was a huge gilded clock. And statues of angels — the most beautiful things I'd ever seen!

Then we emerged onto a bustling city street.

"Wow!" we exclaimed again. People were everywhere. Old cars darted along the cobblestone street. Vendors were selling apples and newspapers, flowers and roasted chestnuts!

We stumbled along the sidewalk with our mouths hanging open.

Suddenly, I stopped and shook my head. "Ethel," I said, "I almost forgot why we're here. We have to find this Mr. Hicks."

I grabbed her hand and we walked to a corner flower stall. An old, witchy woman sat inside. Irritably, she kept rearranging her wares — sad-looking daisies, day-old roses and faded carnations.

"Um, excuse me," I said. "We are looking for a jeweler. A man named Mr. Hicks. Do you know where his shop is?"

"Hicks, eh?" the old woman drawled, opening a mouth with more spaces in it than teeth. "What do you want with him? The man's batty! His shop's been closed for years!"

My heart leapt into my throat. No! Mr. Hicks was my last chance!

"Do you know if . . . if he still lives in Lexington?" I squeaked.

"Oh, he still has an apartment over his old shop, about half a mile that-a-way," the woman replied, pointing. "He's on Carter Street."

"Thank you," I breathed, tugging at Ethel's sleeve. We were just about to cross the street when the flower seller squawked at us.

"I'd think hard before I visited old man Hicks," she called. "He's feeble. Doddering. Can't get out to buy gems anymore. I hear he substitutes with the teeth of kiddies!"

She cackled, opening her gap-toothed mouth wide.

"I wonder if she learned that from experience," I whispered. But I didn't wait around to ask.

We were off to find Mr. Hicks.

Chapter Thirty-Four

"Hey look," Ethel cried as we tromped up Carter Street. "I think that's it."

She was pointing at a storefront. A padlock hung on the front door. The window was boarded up. The sign sagged. It said, "Hicks Fine Gems and Jewelry. Est. 1880."

"The flower seller wasn't kidding," I moaned. "This place has been closed forever."

"Yeah, but she said he lived in an apartment above the store," Ethel said. "Here's a stairwell."

The stairs were next to the shop's door. We peered up the long passageway.

"Dark," I observed.

"Do you think he's up there?" Ethel asked.

"Only one way to find out," I said. I started climbing the stairs. Ethel tiptoed behind me.

Blue paint was chipping off the door at the top of the stairwell. There was no bell. Timidly, I knocked.

We waited. My stomach churned.

There was no answer. I turned to Ethel and shrugged.

"Maybe we should get out of here," she whispered. "I've got the willies, bad!"

"Me, too," I squeaked.

I had taken a single step down the stairs when the door burst open.

I stared up at an extremely tall old man. His beard was long and yellow-white. His shoulders were rounded. His clothes — faded, but clean — hung loosely on his skinny frame.

"What?" the man barked. "What are you selling? Whatever it is, I don't want none. Now *git*, ya varmints."

He leaned down and thrust his face into mine. His breath smelled like . . . chocolate! "Or," he said, "should I call the cops?"

Chapter Thirty-Five

"Please, Mr. Hicks!" I quavered. "You are Mr. Hicks, aren't you?"

"Maybe," the man said, straightening up. He glared at me with cloudy blue eyes that reminded me of Mamaw.

"Miss Montgomery sent us," I said.

"Don't know her," he said, scowling.

"Yes, you must," Ethel cried. "Miss Jane Montgomery. Our schoolteacher. She said you were a friend of the family."

"Oh," Mr. Hicks said quietly. "Oh yes. Janie Montgomery. Sweet girl. With long red hair?"

"That's her!" I exclaimed.

"How . . . how is the poor girl?" he asked softly.

"Oh, she's splendiferous," Ethel gushed. "She's the best teacher for miles around Bearhead Holler. And she has a very nice beau. Jonathan Hughes. He owns the general store."

Relief seemed to spread across Mr. Hicks' face. He opened his shabby door wide.

"Come in," he said. "I'm sorry for my gruffness. Sometimes kids — they come and bang on my door. They call me names and tease me. I thought you were a couple of them. But of course you're not. Come, come, have some chocolates."

He thrust a box of bon-bons at us. Ethel and I each grabbed a piece of candy and sat down on a couple of ripped-up leather chairs.

"So, what can I do for you?" Mr. Hicks asked.

I handed him the lump of coal.

Mr. Hicks slipped on a pair of funny glasses with a tiny telescope sticking out of each lens. I covered my mouth to keep from laughing.

"Hmmm," he grunted as he examined the coal. "Humph."

He turned to his desk, which was littered with small, dusty tools.

He chiseled a gray rock out of the coal lump. Then he held the rock up to a tiny round blade that he set to whirring with a foot pedal. With a horrible sawing sound and a few expert swipes, Mr. Hicks turned that ugly gray rock into a clear sparkling stone.

"Where did you find these diamonds?" Mr. Hicks exclaimed.

Ethel and I jumped out of our chairs.

"There really *are* diamonds in my daddy's corn field," I shouted.

"Your daddy's corn field!" Mr. Hicks exclaimed. He threw his head back and laughed.

"I'll be doggone!" he crowed. "Well, it's not unheard of. Legend has it that once every generation or so, diamonds do crop up in these Appalachian Mountains. Just like this — nesting in a seam of coal."

"So will you help me, Mr. Hicks?" I asked. "Will you come back to Bearhead Holler and tell my parents that these are really diamonds?"

I explained how Spindler and Ratzman would practically steal our fortune away from us the very next day if my parents couldn't be convinced.

But Mr. Hicks' shoulders sagged.

"Oh no, I couldn't do that," he said. "I'm an old man, too old to travel. Besides, I've vowed never again to meddle.

"The last time I got mixed up in other folks' affairs, I ruined a girl's life. Or so I thought," he said. "I made a diamond ring for a powerful old man, even though I knew his fiancé was being forced into the engagement by her father. Chased that girl right out of Lexington — her home."

Ethel and I gulped. He was talking about Miss Montgomery! Still, I couldn't resist one more try.

"Oh, *please*, sir," I said. "Isn't there any way you could help?"

"Well, I can give you documentation," he said. He rifled through a desk drawer and pulled out a form.

"This here is a certificate of authenticity," he said, scribbling on the form. "I authorize that this is a genuine diamond worth, let's see, one thousand dollars!"

I gasped.

"Yup, it's astonishing, isn't it?" he said. "Who

knows? There could be millions stashed away in your daddy's cornfield. Tell your parents that, as a certified gem expert, I'd advise them not to sell their land until every stone is dug up."

Chapter Thirty-Six

Before we left Mr. Hicks' apartment, Ethel insisted on sewing the cut diamond and the certificate into the hem of my skirt.

"This is too important to let it go falling out of your pocket," she said.

As soon as she made the last stitch, I shouted, "OK, let's go! We don't have a minute to waste. We've got to beat those speculators back to my mama and daddy."

We thanked Mr. Hicks quickly and high-tailed it for the train station. In no time, the train for Bearhead Holler was in sight.

"It'll be so much nicer sneaking onto the train when it's not moving," I whispered to Ethel as we hurried down the boardwalk beside the train. On the other side of us was the fancy train station, as well as a row of shops and hotels.

"You said it," she giggled.

"Hey, there's an empty boxcar," I said. "Here Ethel, give me a boost and then I'll pull you up."

Ethel was shoving me into the boxcar when a shrill *Tweet* pierced the air. Then a male voice rang out. "Hey you little hoboes! You wanna ride the train, you can buy a ticket!"

I peered over my shoulder and spotted an angry policeman heading straight for us!

"Whoa!" I shrieked. "It's a cop! Run Ethel, run!"

She dropped me to the ground with a thud and darted off.

Rude!

"I meant run *with* me, not *from* me!" I called. I scrambled to my feet and followed her.

Tweet, tweet! went the policeman's whistle. "Stop those little freeloaders," he shouted.

But we were too fast for him. Ethel and I dove into a crowd of travelers bustling down the boardwalk. In two seconds we slipped out the other side. There was no way for the policeman to see us through the crowd of grown-ups.

"Quick," Ethel yelled. "In here."

We jumped through the first doorway we came to.

We found ourselves in a dark and smoky room. A player piano was banging out tinny dance music. Sawdust covered the floor. And a line of men stood at a bar, tossing back glasses of whiskey.

"We're in a saloon!" Ethel said. She was awestruck.

"Oh, the preacher would not like this at all!" I whispered.

"Your preacher's not the only one," said a familiar voice behind me. I whirled around.

It was Spindler!

He was carrying a top hat and an ebony walking stick. Right behind him was Ratzman, holding his own cane and cracking his knuckles.

"You know the drill," I yelled at Ethel.

We ran!

We cut straight through the saloon and out a back door. We found ourselves in an alley. With the evil speculators right behind us!

"Hide!" Ethel shouted.

She jumped into a coal dust bin and pulled the lid shut. I looked around wildly.

There was nowhere to go! In desperation, I leaped onto a fire escape ladder and started climbing.

The speculators burst out of the bar. They didn't see me. But a sly smile curled Spindler's skinny lips. He tapped Ratzman on the shoulder and pointed to the metal dust bin. Ratzman grinned and nodded.

Then they started banging on the bin with their canes.

Ethel started to shriek in terror.

I had to do something!

Chapter Thirty-Seven

With a warrior's howl, I dropped onto Spindler's shoulders. I covered his eyes with one hand and beat on the top of his head with the other.

"Take that!" I yelled. "And that!"

"Oh yeah?" he called. "Take *this*!" He started racing backwards.

"*Oof*!" I grunted. Spindler had slammed me into the brick wall of the alley. I felt dizzy and limp.

Spindler was reaching up to grab me! I was too shaken to fight. I felt hands gripping my waist.

But the hands didn't belong to Spindler.

Suddenly, I was whizzing backwards! I flew through a window. And then I was standing — safe — in a hotel room!

I whirled around.

"Mr. Hicks!" I cried.

But he didn't have time to say hello. As soon as I made it through the window, Mr. Hicks leaned back out into the alley. He was gripping a heavy board, which he brought down on Spindler's head with a *thunk*.

Spindler fell in a heap.

Ratzman was still beating on the dust bin. But when he saw his partner collapsed on the ground, his pudgy face went scarlet.

"Why you . . . " Ratzman yelled. He rushed to the window with his fist cocked. Almost casually, Mr. Hicks thunked him on the head, too.

Plop! Down he went.

Mr. Hicks turned to me. His blue eyes had lost their cloudiness. In fact, they almost sparkled. I gave him a big bear hug.

"You saved my life!" I said.

"A lucky thing my meddling instincts returned," Mr. Hicks said. "After you girls left me, I decided I'd better make sure you got on the train OK."

I slapped my forehead. "Ethel!"

Mr. Hicks and I rushed down to the street in front of the saloon. We ran smack into Ethel. She was black with coal dust.

"Are you OK?" I asked.

"Y-y-yeah," she stuttered. "Just sh-shook up."

Mr. Hicks pointed into the alley. "Uh, girls, I think we'd better go now. Your speculator friends are waking up."

Spindler and Ratzman were shaking their heads and struggling to their feet. "Hey," yelled Ratzman, "There they are. Let's get 'em!"

We dashed down the boardwalk. The speculators started after us. When we made it to the train's caboose, I peeked behind me.

"Hey, where'd they go?" I called. The three of

us skidded to a stop. We peered into the crowd.

There they were! Spindler and Ratzman hadn't lost us — they had given up on us!

Instead of chasing us, they hopped onto the train. It was chugging out of the depot. We'd never catch it!

"Oh no!" I wailed. "We got rid of the speculators. But we also missed the train. They'll beat us to Bearhead Holler for sure now!"

"Not if I can help it!" said Mr. Hicks.

Chapter Thirty-Eight

"Wh-what do you mean?" I asked.

"How do you think I got here so fast?" Mr. Hicks asked. He grabbed my hand. He grabbed Ethel's. Then he dragged us to the street in front of train station.

"Ladies," he announced. "There's more than one way to get to Bearhead Holler!" He pointed proudly to a dusty, rusty, old-timey car!

"Wow," Ethel exclaimed. She scrambled into the convertible's threadbare front seat. "Where'd you get this old thing? This is a 1908 Model T!"

"I got this automobile from an oil man," Mr. Hicks said, kneeling in front of the car. He started cranking a handle around and around. "He traded it to me for an emerald bracelet. Hop in, Betty!"

I climbed into the back seat just as the Model T coughed to a start. The car lurched backward. It chugged forward. It puttered slowly down the street.

"We'll never make it," I groaned to myself. Over the loud sputtering of the engine, Mr. Hicks didn't hear me.

Instead he shouted, "Yup! Still works like a charm! We'll be there in no time!"

Chapter Thirty-Nine

We'd been poking along a long, winding road for a good forty-five minutes.

"Thank you again for rescuing us, Mr. Hicks," I called from the back seat. Then I added nervously, "Um, how much further to Bearhead Holler, do you think?"

"I'd guess about a hundred miles," he yelled cheerfully. "Ah, smell that air. I did forget how much I enjoy a drive through the country."

Ethel looked back at me with alarm in her eyes. I shook my head desperately. She turned to Mr. Hicks.

"I don't want to sound ungrateful," Ethel said. "But at the rate we're going, I don't think we're going to make it on time."

"Oh, yes we will," Mr. Hicks declared. "You see, girls, there's something you don't know about me. I didn't always live in the big city. I grew up in a holler, too. Camp Creek Holler."

"That's right next door to Bearhead!" I exclaimed.

"Uh-huh," Mr. Hicks replied. "And if there's one thing every holler kid knows, it's . . . "

"Short-cuts!" Ethel and I shouted.

"You got it," called our driver. He turned the steering wheel sharply to the right. Suddenly, we were racing down a narrow, rocky road.

Speeding to Bearhead Holler!

Chapter Forty

We were making great time when Mr. Hicks suddenly slammed on the brakes.

"What happened?" I asked. "Why'd you stop?"

Ethel pointed in front of the car. *"B-b-bear!"* she hissed. "It's blocking our way!"

"Just stay calm, Ethel dear," Mr. Hicks said. "Nobody move. I have just the thing for that grizzly. Works every time."

Slowly, Mr. Hicks opened the glove box. He rummaged around for a second and then he pulled out — a diamond! A big one!

"Bear!" he called out. "Hey bear!"

The woolly beast wagged its head at us. Mr. Hicks held the jewel up so it glinted in the light of the setting sun. The bear stopped. It cocked its head. It growled a little.

"Here ya go," Mr. Hicks yelled. Then he threw the diamond to the side of the road!

The bear lumbered after its shiny prize. It was out of our way.

Mr. Hicks slammed his foot on the gas and we sped off.

"Mr. Hicks," I exclaimed. "Y-you just gave that bear a diamond! And if my little diamond is worth a thousand dollars, that big one must have been worth five thousand!"

Mr. Hicks threw back his head and laughed.

"Glass," he shouted. "Pure rhinestone. You know, bears love pretty, shiny things almost as much as people. It's silly really. That's why I quit the jewelry business. I saw too much silly greed for baubles."

"Then why are you helping me?" I asked.

"Because if there's anything uglier than greed, my dear, it is injustice," said Mr. Hicks. "I *will* see to it that you get your due."

Chapter Forty-One

We drove on as night fell.

We went through Snailback Holler, Hug Betty Narrows and Needmore Township. Somewhere along the way, I drifted off to sleep.

I awoke with a start when I realized the car had stopped.

I blinked and squinted. The sun was just coming up over the green mountaintops. It was beautiful.

Ethel was just waking up too. She rubbed her eyes and gave a huge yawn. "Where are we?" she mumbled.

Suddenly, she sat straight up. "We're home!" she shouted. "We're at the base of Bearhead Holler. Let's keep going Mr. Hicks. Betty's house is the last one on this dirt road."

Mr. Hicks' face was gray and drawn. He shrugged helplessly. "I'm sorry girls," he said. "We're out of gas!"

"No!" I shouted, jumping out of the back seat. "We can't fail now! We've come so far!"

Ethel climbed out of the car after me. "Let's run!"

We started racing up the holler road. But Mr. Hicks was too old and too tired to get anywhere very fast.

"You go on," he huffed. "You've got my document. I'll wait down here with the car."

I didn't want to, but I was about to agree. Then I saw a blond-haired man walking up the road, leading a horse. The animal was weighed down by two canvas sacks stamped "U.S. MAIL."

"That mailman has a horse," I said. "Maybe he'll let us borrow . . . "

"*That mailman*?" the man shouted. "Is that any way to address your favorite Uncle Jack?"

I tried to smile as if I recognized him.

"I'm sorry, Uncle Jack," I babbled, and ran to give him a hug. "I'm so tired, I didn't realize it was you. We've been driving all night, you see. And listen — we need to borrow your horse. I've got to get home, now! It's almost a matter of life and death!"

"Oh, now I don't know," Uncle Jack said, scratching his head. "I was just starting my mail route. And you know the saying, 'Neither rain, nor sleet, nor snow, nor hail, will keep the mailman from his . . . ' *Hey*!"

While Uncle Jack was making excuses to me, Mr. Hicks and Ethel had been sneaking behind his back.

They lifted first one mail sack off the horse and then the other. Then they both climbed on the horse's back.

Mr. Hicks yelled, "Hee-yah!" and the horse began trotting up the road.

I raced after them and hopped onto the horse behind Mr. Hicks.

"Sorry Uncle Jack," I called over my shoulder. "But I promise — if we get home in time, you'll never have to deliver the mail again!"

Chapter Forty-Two

We crashed into my house — only to find Great-grandma and Great-granddaddy sitting at the kitchen table with Spindler and Ratzman!

Great-granddaddy sat hunched over a stack of papers with a pen in his hand.

"Noooo!" I shouted. I leapt to grab the pen away from him.

Great-grandma jumped to her feet. Her face was white. "Betty," she cried. "Where have you been?"

"In Lexington," Ethel answered for me.

I ripped open the hem of my dress. Then I plunked our sparkly, cut diamond and the certificate of authenticity on the table.

"Mr. Hicks here has something to tell you," I said.

Mr. Hicks cleared his throat. "Indeed, I do," he said. "Look at that gem, Mr. and Mrs. Jones. It's a beauty, isn't it? And very valuable. You see, your coal *is* impure, as you feared. But only because it is riddled with diamonds!"

Somberly, Mr. Hicks faced Great-granddaddy.

"I urge you sir," he said. "Don't sell your mineral rights to these swindlers, no matter what they are offering. You've got a *fortune* buried in your land."

My great-grandparents turned on the smarmy speculators.

"You tried to dupe us," Great-grandma whispered, sounding hurt.

"You can take yourselves and your phony contract, and *get off my land*," Great-granddaddy growled. "Now!"

He grabbed the papers and ripped them to pieces!

Spindler brought two gloved fingers to his waxy mustache and gave it a casual twirl. He laughed — a slow, evil laugh. Ratzman stood behind him and cracked his knuckles.

"Oh, you hillbillies," Spindler chuckled. "You're so naive. What you don't understand is those diamonds are ours! *Contract or not!*"

He pulled a pistol from his coat pocket, cocked it and pointed it straight at me.

"Ratzman," he barked. "Lock 'em in the root cellar. *All of 'em!*"

Chapter Forty-Three

So there we were — my great-grandparents, Ethel, Mr. Hicks and me — trapped in a dank, dark cellar with only turnips and onions for company.

"We've got to do something!" I wailed, pacing the dirt floor. "They're up there right now, stealing our fortune. Our *future*!"

Silence filled the cellar like a sour smell. Nobody had any ideas.

We sat there.

Helpless.

I squinched my eyes shut and plopped on the floor to sulk. My mind went hazy. All I could see was blackness. Then the blackness turned gray. And then a picture — faint and shaky — emerged.

I leaped to my feet. "The fox tunnels!" I cried. "Ethel, I'm almost sure of it. A tunnel runs right against the root cellar!"

"Really?" Ethel asked.

"*What* are you talking about?" Great-grandma exclaimed. "Tunnels?"

"Oh, you'd be surprised how many tricks these girls have up their sleeves," Mr. Hicks said with a grin.

"We'll explain later," I shouted. "For now, everybody choose a wall. Start knocking until you hear a hollow sound."

We all started tapping the dirt walls with our knuckles.

After a few minutes, Ethel cried, "I think I found it!" She pointed to a spot near the floor.

Great-granddaddy and Mr. Hicks picked up a couple wooden stools and started bashing the wall. Soon the dirt crumbled.

They had broken through!

I dropped to my knees and stuck my head through the hole. "This is it!" I cried. "This is our fox tunnel."

Great-granddaddy took off his jacket and began to roll up his sleeves. "Thomas, what are you doing?" Great-grandma asked.

"I'm going out there. I'm going to save our fortune!" Great-granddaddy said through gritted teeth.

"You can't," I cried. "You're too big to fit. And besides, only me and Ethel know the way."

Great-granddaddy's face fell. "But this is all our fault," he whispered. "If only your mother and I had trusted you, we wouldn't be in this fix."

A lump rose in my throat. I threw my arms around Great-granddaddy's waist and squeezed hard. He didn't scare me anymore.

I motioned to Ethel.

"Quick," I hissed. "Let's go."

Chapter Forty-Four

Ethel and I crawled through the tunnels.

It was dark. And damp.

And smelly.

And scary!

We made turn after turn. But we weren't hitting the surface.

"Ethel," I whispered. "Do you think we're lost?"

"We might be," she quavered. "The only thing we can do is just keep going 'til we're unlost!"

"What if we never get unlost?" I wailed.

"Don't think about that," Ethel said. "Just move!"

We kept going. We made a twist to the left. A turn to the right. We climbed up a little hill. Then we veered left again.

Just when I was beginning to resign myself to the life of a mole, I saw something up ahead. I squinted.

"What's that?" I said. "It's glowing!"

"It's sunlight," Ethel cried. "We're free!" We raced to the light. It was shining through a wide hole in the ground. We climbed up to find ourselves in a field of some sort. We lay on our backs, gasping with relief.

"Fresh air!" I cried, sucking in a big breath.

"Where are we?" Ethel asked.

I got to my feet to look around. Then I gasped and ducked back down.

"Oh no!" I hissed. "We're in Daddy's cornfield! And the speculators are a hundred feet away, digging like crazy! How are we going to stop them?"

"I don't know," Ethel wailed.

"Hey!" It was Spindler's voice, dripping venom. "Who's out there?"

The speculators started crashing through the corn stalks.

"It's those meddling girls!" Ratzman yelled. "Let's get 'em!"

Chapter Forty-Five

"*Noooo!*" I cried.

Before we could get our bearings, I ran off in one direction and Ethel ran off in another. In a few seconds, she was out of sight.

The speculators turned their attention to me.

I ran as fast as I'd ever run in my life. I didn't even pay attention to where I was going. My feet had a mind of their own.

I heard Spindler pant, "She's heading to the mine!"

Indeed I was. In a minute, I was in my secret hiding place. My cave. For an instant, I even felt comforted.

But then Spindler and Ratzman invaded my secret place.

"Grab her!" Spindler shouted.

Ratzman lunged at me. Just before his meaty paws closed around my neck, I ducked and he flew over me and hit the cave's rocky wall. "*Oof!*" he grunted. "Rotten kid!"

Spindler lurched towards me. I dropped to all fours and scrambled between his legs, tripping him. He fell to the ground with a thump.

"Dodge and weave all you like, little girl," he snarled. "But there's two of us and one of you. We'll catch you all right. And then it's *into the mine shaft!*"

He pointed at the yawning mouth of the mine. I screamed and darted off again.

But as they chased me around the cave, I remembered something. That hole! The emergency exit I'd almost fallen into when I first morphed!

Spindler and Ratzman couldn't know about it.

I twisted around and started running for the hole as fast as I could.

"After her!" Spindler called. Ratzman was puffing behind me. Spindler was puffing behind him.

I spied the hole. I hoped the speculators didn't see it too!

At the last possible moment before I would have plunged into the emergency exit, I jumped.

I sailed over the hole and crashed to the ground on the opposite side. I whipped around just in time to see Ratzman tumble down the shaft.

"*Whoooaaaa!*" he bellowed.

Spindler skidded to a stop. His toes were dangling over the shaft. He flapped his arms wildly. Just as I had that first day, he leaned backward.

And he leaned forward.

Then he fell in!

"*Arrrrrgh!*" Plop. He must have landed right on Ratzman.

Groans and grunts floated up the shaft. "Oh,

my arm's broken for sure!" one of them said.

"That's nothing. I think I've broken both my legs," said the other.

I collapsed in relief. "Safe at last!" I breathed.

"Oh really?" said a growly voice.

I stared at the mouth of the cave.

"Clemmmmm!"

Chapter Forty-Six

"You're not getting away this time!" Clem snarled.

As I tried to dash past him, he grabbed me and lifted me over his head. Then he lumbered to the emergency exit.

He was going to throw me down there with the speculators!

"Oh, no you don't," I yelled. I started kicking my legs wildly. I beat on Clem's woolly head with my fists. Clem stumbled and spun around.

With a roar, he threw me from his arms.

Crack!

Pain shot through my left leg. My eyes flew open. I expected to find myself heaped on top of the speculators. But I wasn't.

When I was kicking at Clem, my legs must have gotten tangled up in the cable ladder! Then when he dropped me, I was left dangling upside-down from the cables.

"Ooowwww!" I gasped. "My leg! It's broken!"

"That's not all that's gonna be broken when I get you off that ladder," Clem yelled, lunging at me. I was too weak with pain to fend him off.

Suddenly, I heard a voice yell, "Freeze! Police!"

Clem's eyes went buggy. He made one last grab for me. But he was so startled by the shout of the policeman that he lost his footing.

"H-h-help!" he screeched as he plunged into the hole. I heard a sickening thud and then *three* sets of groans rose from the shaft.

I squinted at the mouth of the cave. There was Uncle Jack, wearing a gold badge and holding a gun.

"Uncle Jack," I said. "You're the holler mailman *and* the policeman?"

"Gotta stay busy," Uncle Jack said, winking at me. "Ethel came and got me. We got your folks out of the root cellar. Then, luckily, Ethel thought to come here. She said it was your secret hiding place. Looks like we got here just in time."

"Wow," I whispered, wincing in pain. "This was Mamaw's secret hiding place, too!"

Behind Uncle Jack, I could see Ethel jumping up and down in excitement. Mr. Hicks was beaming. And Great-granddaddy and Great-grandma were coming towards me.

"Oh Betty dear," Great-grandma called, her arms outstretched. "We're going to get you down from there right now! Everything's going to be all right!"

Her voice sounded far away. I felt woozy. Suddenly, the scent of almonds enveloped me. Then everything went black!

<u>Chapter Forty-Seven</u>

I was staring at the roof of the cave. Blinking. My eyelids felt heavy. My whole *body* felt heavy.

"What . . . happened?" I groaned.

Like an evening fog, the memory came to me.

I had saved my family's fortune from the speculators — and almost gotten killed in the process. Luckily, I'd escaped with only a broken leg.

The memory of that pain made me start. I sat up. I looked down at my leg. It looked . . . strange.

Not only was it whole and unbroken, but my drop-waisted dress and my high-ankled boots had disappeared.

Instead I was wearing clean, new jeans that fit perfectly. I also had on a pretty purple sweater and sturdy sneakers I'd never seen before.

"What?" I murmured. I creaked to my feet. I looked around. Once again, the mineshaft was boarded up!

On impulse, I grabbed a hank of my hair and peered at the ends. It was blond!

I had morphed back to myself. I was Amy again! Amy with better clothes, that is!

There on the ground next to my feet was the

"Hillbilly Witchery" book! I grabbed it and flipped to the return-morph potion.

Next to a list of ingredients, I spotted these instructions:

"If from your morph, you want to flee
Simply mix this recipe
But if the brew is out of sight,
Just wait until the time is right!"

I dashed out of the cave and headed home. I bounded up the steps and noticed that the porch rail held flowerpots and the rockers were sturdy and comfortable — just as they'd been in 1920.

I burst through the door. "Mama? Daddy? Jud?" I called. Nobody was there.

I gazed around. The cabin sure looked different. It was fresh-scrubbed and sunny. And it was filled with colorful crafts and hand-carved wood furniture.

But where was everybody?

"Where is Mamaw?" I said in a panic.

"Hello? Hello? Who's there?" I heard a vaguely familiar voice calling from the front porch. Then somebody's head poked through the front door.

"Mamaw!" I shrieked, running over to her. "You look . . . so good!" I exclaimed.

"Why thank you, sweetheart," Mamaw said, stepping into the house. I noticed she had a slight limp. And she was favoring her left leg. The one I had broken!

Other than that, she looked wonderful. I barely recognized her. Her hair was a soft brown. Her eyes were blue and sparkling. Her voice wasn't creaky or croaky in the slightest.

She seemed twenty years younger than the last time I'd seen her!

She was dressed in jeans and hiking boots and holding a beautiful, carved walking stick.

"Mamaw, what are you doing up? You were so sick," I said.

"I was? Are you sure you didn't dream that?" Mamaw asked with a glint in her eye. "I'm feeling great. I was just using the walking stick your daddy carved for me — taking my daily constitutional around the grounds."

Grounds? What was she talking about?

"The real question, young lady," Mamaw said, "is what are you doing out here in the guest house?"

Chapter Forty-Eight

Guest house?

I was speechless. I stumbled outside with Mamaw and followed her behind the "guest house."

I gazed around me. I was surrounded by huge, beautiful trees and patches of meadow.

"Wh-where is the corn field?" I stuttered.

"Corn field?" Mamaw said. "Why you've never seen corn stalks here. There hasn't been corn here since I was twelve. We dug it up to mine the diamonds. You know that."

"Oh, yeah," I said. I was trembling. A thrill shot up my spine.

"After they dug up all the gems, your great-granddaddy planted these trees," Mamaw said. "Over the years, it has become a right pretty orchard, hasn't it?"

"Oh, yes," I breathed.

"The children sure like it," Mamaw said as she tromped along.

"Children?" I asked.

"Why yes, darling," Mamaw said with a laugh. "You know, you can't have a school without school children!"

She pointed across the meadow to an elegant brick building I'd never seen before. A sign hanging over the front steps said, "The Jane Montgomery Hughes Memorial School."

"Wow," I whispered. "I guess Miss Montgomery found true love after all!"

I gazed around the school grounds. Kids were everywhere. Looking plump and healthy, they sat against trees and on the school steps. Most of them were reading books! Even William Mott!

"E-everybody looks so healthy," I marveled. "So well-fed. And they're reading!"

"Well, yes," Mamaw remarked. "It's all because of your great-granddaddy!"

"Really?" I said. "Tell me about it!"

"Well you know, not too long after we discovered our diamond mine, the Depression struck," Mamaw recalled. "And our family just did everything we could. It began with food and housing. But then we started improving the schools and the roads.

"My Uncle Jack — remember him? He lived to be 103!" Mamaw exclaimed. "Anyway, Uncle Jack gave up his mail route and went to college. He learned about agriculture and business. When he came back to Bearhead, he taught the holler people to terrace their fields and fight erosion. And he convinced a lot of folks — your daddy the master whittler included — to sell their crafts.

"Now Bearhead Holler is known for its pottery, quilts and oak baskets," Mamaw said. "People here had no idea how valuable our old mountain crafts were! But now everybody *does* agree — Bearhead Holler has become a paradise in these mountains!"

I was stunned.

And when we came to a tall, beautiful Victorian house, my mouth dropped open. The house was painted a sunny yellow and it had a huge, white, wraparound front porch.

"Is this our house?" I asked.

Mamaw laughed. "Well you know it is! You've lived here all your life!"

My daddy was sitting in a rocker on the porch, carving wood. Mama was there too — popping beans. Both looked much happier and younger than I'd ever seen them look!

"Amy, there you are honey," Mama called. "I've laid out a nice after-school snack for you in the kitchen."

I bounded up the stairs and gave Mama and Daddy kisses hello. They acted like that was the most normal thing in the world.

Then I ran inside.

My house was beautiful! Everywhere you looked there were colorful quilts hanging on the walls and face jugs grinning from bookshelves.

In the kitchen, there was cool, running water — no pump! On a pretty, hand-woven place mat, my mother had set out a bunch of fresh fruit and some molasses cookies.

I gazed around me. Instantly, I felt right at home.

Clearly my family wasn't "fancy rich" like I'd read about in books — all velvet and lace and formality. Instead, the Jones house was filled with the art of the holler and with homey comforts.

I sighed happily. Everything was going to be all right!